SUMMER
READING
AWARD

in Honor of

READASAURUS

BRIAN HARRIS

1988

James Prendergast Library Association
509 Cherry Street Jamestown NY 14701

The Big Fat Worm

by NANCY VAN LAAN
Pictures by MARISABINA RUSSO

ALFRED A. KNOPF 🐎 NEW YORK

For Anna, David, and Jennifer — N.V.L.

For Whitney — M.R.

THIS IS A BORZOI BOOK PUBLISHED BY ALFRED A. KNOPF, INC.

Text copyright © 1987 by Nancy Van Laan. Illustrations copyright © 1987 by Marisabina Russo.
All rights reserved under International and Pan-American Copyright Conventions. Published in the
United States by Alfred A. Knopf, Inc., New York, and simultaneously in Canada by Random House of
Canada Limited, Toronto. Distributed by Random House, Inc., New York.
Manufactured in Singapore   10 9 8 7 6 5 4 3 2 1

Library of Congress Cataloging-in-Publication Data
Van Laan, Nancy. The big fat worm. Summary: A rhythmic read-aloud describing a chain of events set
in motion when a big fat bird tries to eat a big fat worm. [1. Worms—Fiction.   2. Birds—Fiction.
3. Animals—Fiction]   I. Russo, Marisabina, ill.   II. Title.   PZ7.V263Bi   1987   [E]   86-20158
ISBN 0-394-88763-8   ISBN 0-394-98763-2 (lib. bdg.)

A big fat bird found a big fat worm

and the big fat bird said HI WORM

and the big fat worm said HI BIRD

and the big fat bird said
I'M GOING TO EAT YOU UP

and the big fat worm said
OH NO YOU'RE NOT

and the big fat bird said
OH YES I AM

and the worm said NO
and the bird said YES

and the worm disappeared down a hole in the ground . . .

when along came a big fat cat.
The big fat cat said HI BIRD

and the big fat bird said HI CAT
and the big fat cat said
I'M GOING TO EAT YOU UP

and the big fat bird said
OH NO YOU'RE NOT

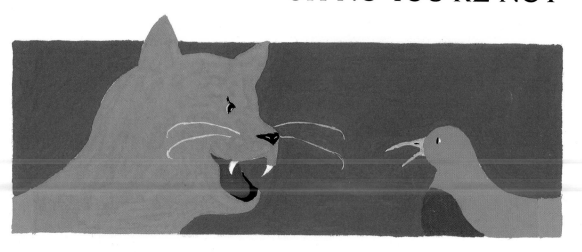

and the big fat cat said
OH YES I AM

and the bird said NO
and the cat said YES

and the bird flew far far away . . .

when along came a big fat dog.
The big fat dog said HI CAT

and the big fat cat said
HI DOG

and the big fat dog said
I'M GOING TO EAT YOU UP

and the big fat cat said
OH NO YOU'RE NOT

and the big fat dog said
OH YES I AM

and the cat said NO
and the dog said YES

and the cat scooted up a tall tall tree.

So the big fat dog ran all the way home

where he dug and he dug and he pulled up a bone
and he chewed and he chewed and he chewed.

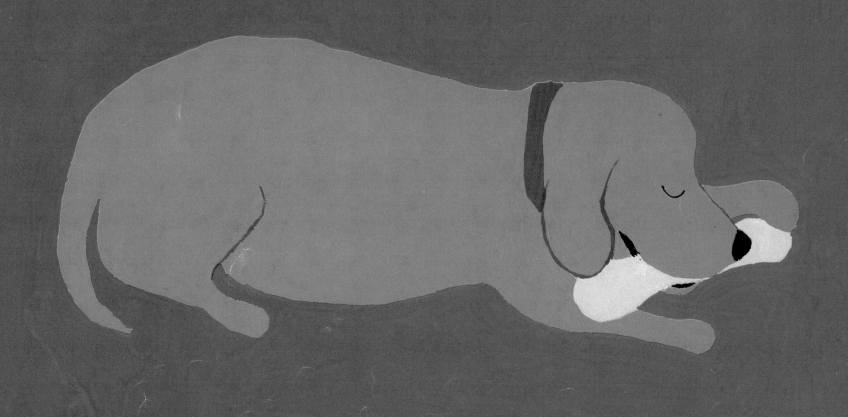

And the big fat cat came down to the ground
and he looked all around and he walked all around
and he yawned and he fell sound asleep.

Then the big fat bird spinning round and around
flying high in the sky swooped down to the ground

where she found something big,

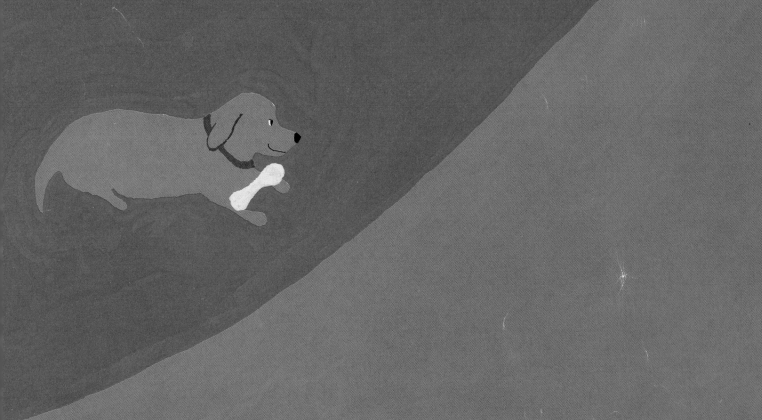

something fat,

something round

and the big fat bird said HI WORM!

STORYTIME   C 01

E
Van Laan, Nancy.   C. 2
    The big fat worm

                                    11·32

DATE DUE

MAR 3 0 1993		